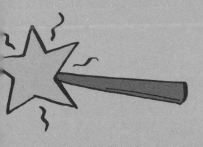

Bedtime Stories

footy

Wanda-Linda Goes Berserk

This book is dedicated to Dunty

A word about wombats: real hairy-nosed wombats don't live with little girls, they live in the bush. If you would like to help wombats such as the threatened Northern Hairy-nosed Wombat, you can help try to protect the places where wombats live. World Wide Fund for Nature Australia, GPO Box 528, Sydney, NSW 2001. The Australian Conservation Foundation Land Clearing Campaign, 340 Gore Street, Fitzroy, Victoria 3065.

Viking

Published by the Penguin Group
Penguin Books Australia Ltd
250 Camberwell Road, Camberwell, Victoria 3124, Australia
Penguin Books Ltd
80 Strand, London WC2R 0RL, England
Penguin Putnam Inc.
375 Hudson Street, New York, New York 10014, USA
Penguin Books, a division of Pearson Canada
10 Alcorn Avenue, Toronto, Ontario, Canada M4V 3B2
Penguin Books (NZ) Ltd
Cnr Rosedale and Airborne Roads, Albany, Auckland, New Zealand
Penguin Books (South Africa) (Pty) Ltd
24 Sturdee Avenue, Rosebank, Johannesburg 2196, South Africa
Penguin Books India (P) Ltd
11, Community Centre, Panchsheel Park, New Delhi 110 017, India

First published by Penguin Books Australia Ltd 2002

10 9 8 7 6 5 4 3 2 1

Designed by Tony Palmer, Penguin Design Studio
Typeset in 22 pt Cochin
Scanning and separations by Typescan
Printed and bound in Singapore by Imago Productions

National Library of Australia
Cataloguing-in-Publication data:

Cooke, Kaz, 1962– .
    Wanda-Linda goes berserk.

    ISBN 0 670 88805 2.

    1. Temper tantrums in children – Juvenile fiction.
    I. Title.

A823.3

www.penguin.com.au

WANDA-LINDA goes "BERSERK"

Written and Illustrated by

Kaz Cooke

VIKING

This morning I got out on the
wrong side of the bed.
That's what they call it when you
wake up grumpy.

As you probably know,
my name is Wanda-Linda.
And this is Glenda,
my hairy-nosed wombat.

As usual Glenda woke up
feeling really cheerful.

Glenda tried to make me feel better
by doing a before-breakfast dance,
but I just wasn't in the mood.

'Wanda-Linda, you're carrying on like a pork chop,'
said my mum. 'What's the matter with you today?'

'I don't KNOW,' I said. 'I'm growly
and glary and grouchy.
I'm crabby and cranky and CROSS.'

'You're a bit ratty this morning, Wanda-Linda,'
said my dad. 'What's the matter?'

'Look, I'm talking on the PHONE,'
I shouted at him, 'so shut RIGHT UP!'

I had to have Time Out
before our walk.

On the way through the park
we met Mrs Kafoops.

'Goodness gracious, Wanda-Linda,
what's the matter with you?' she asked.

I made a very rude noise.

'Hell's bells,' said Mrs Kafoops,
'what a beastly crosspatch!'

'If I had my way, she'd be sent straight to bed without any tea,' said Mrs Kafoops.

'We don't do that sort of thing any more,' said Mum.

'What do you do instead?'

'We go right out of our minds,' said Mum.

So I showed The Terrible Underpants.

I rather thought it was time for an ice-cream.
Mum said no.

Well. I went *berserk*.

I lay on the ground and kicked my legs
and ROARED.

Then I ran around and screamed
and stuck my head in a fence,
and it wouldn't come out.
Not even when Mrs Kafoops
put butter on my neck.

Lots of nice, strong firefighters came,
with their siren on, to rescue me.
It was quite a kerfuffle.

Mrs Kafoops went a bit berserk,
but she didn't stick her head in anything.

After the rescue, all the firefighters had to go.

Mum said to remember our manners.
She said thank you, and I told them I was very sorry
for getting my head stuck.

Glenda just looked like she'd rather be digging a hole.

When we got home,
Mum thought a bath might calm things down.

'Wanda-Linda, what was the matter with you today?'
Glenda asked.

And I said, 'Actually, Glenda, I can't remember.'

Tomorrow I think I'll be in quite a good mood,
so we might have a trip in a rocket.

THE END

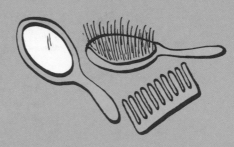

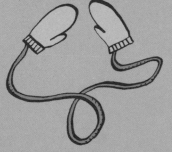